SO-AJF-980

A Horse's Tale

Ten Adventures in One Hundred Years

Edited by
Nancy Luenn

Illustrated by
Connie J. Pope

Authors:
Shanna Stevenson
Roberta Haines
Esther Mumford
Kathryn Armstrong
Judy Laik
Patricia Cochrane
Tim Ryan
Mary Alice Sanguinetti
Chris Gustafson
Peggy King Anderson

Acknowledgements

The publisher would like to thank Patricia Cosgrove at the Burke Museum, Seattle, WA; Sam Shoji with the Japanese-American Citizens Assoc., Seattle, WA; and Karen Bohlke and her staff at El Centro de la Raza, Seattle, WA, for their help and consultation on the manuscript. Thanks also to Nancy Campbell and Sharon Schumacher for their contributions to the design and illustration concept.

Cover designed by Pati Casebolt

Special thanks to language instructor William Charley, who provided us with the Methow term for horse: N'uks-Cha-Ska-Ha.

Copyright © 1989 by Parenting Press Inc.
All rights reserved
ISBN 0-943990-50-5 Paper
ISBN 0-943990-51-3 Library Binding
LC 88-61152

Published by:
Parenting Press, Inc.
P.O. Box 75267
Seattle, WA 98125

Contents

Introduction

You've probably never thought about it before, but toys lead very adventurous lives. At least I have. My name is N'uks-Cha-Ska-Ha. Well, that's the closest you can come in English. You see it is very hard for people to say words in horse language. But most children call me whatever they want—so I guess it doesn't matter.

When I was first carved, I was disappointed to find myself standing on a shelf. I was carved by an old man with wrinkled fingers. He was a woodcarver and made many toys. When he was finished, he put me on the shelf above the fireplace. How dull, I thought. Nothing will happen to me. I'll just stand here forever.

Was I ever wrong! Wait till you hear the tales I have to tell. I've gone to boarding school, and fallen overboard in a storm. I was burned in a fire, and buried under volcanic ash. You can follow my travels on the map on the next page. But, I'm getting ahead of myself.

I had been standing on the shelf for a few weeks, when the old man took me down and wrapped me in paper. Although I didn't know it, he was sending me to his grandson, William. And that is when the fun began . . . .

Washington

Mt. Baker

Skagit River

SAN
JUAN
ISLANDS

Strait of Juan de Fuca

Darrington

OLYMPIC

Everett

Seattle

PENINSULA

Pacific Ocean

Tacoma

Puyallup

Roslyn

C
A
S
C
A
D
E

M
O
U
N
T
A
I
N
S

Olympia

Mt. Rainier

Mount
St. Helens

Mount
Adams

Longview

Vancouver

Colum

O R E G O

0   30 Miles
0   50 Kilometers

The Travels of

State

N
W ← → E
S

Lake Chelan

River

Columbia

GRAND
COULEE
DAM

Mason City

Roosevelt Lake

Spokane River

Spokane

Wenatchee River

Wenatchee

Malaga
Creek

Moses
Lake

Ritzville

Yakima

Snake River

BLUE
MOUNTAINS

River

'uks-Cha-Ska-Ha
he Horse of many adventures

1

1890's

The Tall Wheat
William's Story

It was harvest time. The sky shone bright blue, but where I stood near the threshing machine the dust and chaff were so thick I could hardly see. The steam-powered threshing machine was like a monster. It swallowed the heads of grain and spit out kernels of wheat and flying chaff. The chaff stuck to my hair and face and clothes.

I climbed onto one of the nearby mountains of sacked grain. From the top I could see the mill wagons coming to fetch the bags of wheat. I watched the straw wagon carry away the stalks and outer shells of wheat called chaff. Teams of huge horses pulled the wagons.

"I wish I could drive a wagon," I told my wooden horse, Patch.

"William!" My mother called from the cook wagon. Her voice was cross. Slowly, I climbed down the mountain of grain. Another chore! During harvest all my mother ever says to me is "Do this, do that." She never says "Please."

As I passed the threshing machine, my father looked up from his work. His face was black with dust. "Go and

By Shanna Stevenson

help your mother, son."

"Why can't I help at the threshing machine instead?" I asked. "I could drive the straw wagon."

My father frowned. "That's dangerous work, William. You're too young."

"But I'm not. I'm almost eleven."

My father glared and I made a dash for the cook wagon. He gives orders to fifteen men during harvest and won't take an argument from anyone, least of all me.

The cook wagon stood in the harvested fields, away from the dust thrown by the threshing machine. It was a small house on wheels with an iron stove at one end. Pots, pans and dishes were stacked on benches and everywhere along the sides.

I climbed the steps and went inside. The air in the cookhouse was even hotter than it was outside. Mother was taking more loaves of bread out of the cookstove oven. My mother isn't very pretty during harvest. Her hair was damp from the heat and her long dress and apron were spotted with flour. She looked up with a frown.

"Fill the water barrel, William," she said. "And no grumbling now!"

Shuffling my feet, I went back outside. "It isn't fair," I told Patch. During harvest, my wooden horse was the only friend I had.

I picked up two buckets and started toward Rooster Creek. Waves of heat rose from the ground as I walked. When I have to carry water, I wish I was back in Illinois.

My family moved to Ritzville, Washington, when I was eight. We took the train. Our farm equipment and work horses traveled with us in a box car. I had to leave my best friend and my pony Patch behind. But Grandfather Bill carved me my wooden horse, Patch, and he looks just like my old pony.

It was a long walk to Rooster Creek, up one hill and down into the next hollow. "I wish you were a real horse, Patch," I said. Fetching water wouldn't be so bad if I could ride across the rolling hills.

Our farm in Washington has lots of hills. It is much bigger than our old farm, and my father had to buy more horses. At harvest, horses push the header that cuts the standing grain. They pull the wagons and haul the steam-powered threshing machine. As soon as Father will let me, I'm going to work with the horses.

I scrambled down the slope to Rooster Creek. At this time of year, it was only a trickle. I walked along the bank until I found a pool where I could fill the buckets.

Slowly, I walked back uphill. The full buckets were very heavy. As I walked, the grain stalks caught under my pant legs, scratching my ankles.

Back at the cook wagon, I emptied the buckets into the water barrel. Then I started back toward Rooster Creek. It took three trips, but at last the barrel was full. I dropped the empty buckets and sat down on one of the long benches.

"William!" My mother called from inside the cookhouse. "Set the table, now."

Grumbling to Patch, I went to set the table. My mother isn't very nice during harvest. She never smiles or tells me stories. It's like she is a different person.

I finished setting out the plates just as the men came in from the fields. They were covered with dust and looked hot and tired. But I still wished I could work in the fields.

The men sat at long tables outside while my mother

and I served them heaps of steaming food. When they were finished, Mother and I ate. Then it was time for dishes.

We heated kettles of water on the wood stove to fill big metal dishpans sitting outside on the benches. There were mountains of dishes and silverware to clean before Mother could start to cook dinner. And I would have more chores!

As we worked, Mother didn't say a thing. She just stared out at the tall fields of wheat. When the last plate was dry, I picked up Patch.

"Come on, boy," I whispered. When my mother wasn't looking, I headed for the far field. The tall wheat was my favorite hideout. Once I reached the field, no one could see me.

Patch and I lay down in the wheat. The long stalks grew high above my head. All I could see were the sky and the waving heads of wheat.

"Maybe next year I'll get to drive a wagon," I said to Patch. "By then, maybe I'll convince Father I'm old enough."

I imagined myself sitting on the wagon box with the reins in my hands. In front of me I would see the broad backs of four horses. They would be huge and strong. "They'll know I'm in charge," I told Patch. "They'll obey my every pull on the reins."

I closed my hands around imaginary reins. I would wear thick gloves, but I would feel the reins right through the leather.

"Maybe I'll even get to drive a header," I said. I pictured myself, steering the header with my knees. At the front end of the header would be a huge wheel with long, sharp blades. The wheel would spin around as the header moved across the field. The blades would cut the wheat and push it up a moving canvas belt into a wagon. Six horses would push the header. And I would be perched on the frame behind the horses.

"I'll take you with me," I promised Patch. "In my pocket so the men won't tease." Above my head, the wind rustled through the wheat. The air was hot. I was tired. I yawned and closed my eyes.

"Whooshka, whooshka, whooshka." What was that? I looked up, rubbing sleep from my eyes. Again I heard the sound, closer now. "Whooshka, whooshka." I sat up straight. Then I saw it. The spinning sharp wheel of the header was coming right at me. I froze like a rabbit in the grass. Then I bolted.

"Whooshka, whooshka, whooshka!" I scrambled through the wheat, trying to escape that awful sound. The wheat stalks swayed around me. I bounded through the grain, too scared to look back. Finally I stopped running. I was still in one piece. The noise faded. I just stood there for a minute, panting. Then I remembered Patch. Oh, no! Had I lost my only friend?

I ran back through the wheat until I came to the wide swath of cut grain. The horses' hooves had churned the earth, and the ground was a mess of trampled stalks of grain. My heart sank. How would I ever find a little wooden horse?

I searched and searched, pushing aside the broken stubble until my hands were scratched and bleeding. I tossed aside the clods of earth. The breeze grew cooler. It was getting late. Soon it would be time for supper. I knew I was in trouble, but I had to find Patch.

Finally, I spotted his small head. I dug him out as fast as I could. Would he be all right? For a minute, I was afraid to look. I ran my hands over his smooth body. Whew! I opened my eyes. Only a small part of his left

13

hoof was missing. He was all right.

I headed for the cook wagon. My mother turned around when she heard me coming. "William!" she exclaimed. "Where have you been? I had to move the cookhouse by myself."

I stared up at her, still feeling glad I was alive. She looked disappointed instead of angry. Her face looked tired. All of a sudden, I felt bad.

"I'm sorry, Mother," I said. "I really am. It won't happen again." And I meant it, too.

I stayed out of the tall wheat after that. Somehow it didn't seem the same. Patch and I worked hard. We hauled water, washed dishes and helped with the cooking. My mother smiled a little more. And sometimes she even said "Please."

Before the harvest was over, one of the men had to leave. Father hired a girl to help Mother in the cookhouse.

"William," he said one morning. "You've been a big help the last few weeks. I think you're old enough to drive a wagon."

Proudly, I climbed onto the straw wagon. I wore thick gloves but I could feel the reins right through the leather.

"Giddi-yup!" I shouted. The straw wagon began to move. And the four horses obeyed my every pull on the reins. At last I was driving a wagon!

One day, after William had grown up, he put me in a trunk. I couldn't see a thing! But I could hear horses and men shouting and the creak of wagon wheels. After a while I felt a jolt. The trunk burst open and I fell out onto a dusty road. A man with brown skin and long black hair was looking down at me....

2

1900's

Uncle Twin-Star's Gift
Elsie's Story

The heavy puffs of dust rising from the wheels coated the children in the wagon with fine powder. Dust swirled up through the slats in the wagon bed and made it hard to breathe. Elsie was glad for the bandanna she had tied around her mouth and nose. It helped a little. She had been in the wagon since early yesterday morning when the government's Indian Agent came to take her back to the mission school.

Elsie's uncle had seen the wagon coming from his place of prayer. He hurried with the news in time for Elsie and her mother to prepare themselves.

"Oh Mother," Elsie implored, "do I have to go?" She saw the painful answer in her mother's eyes even as she spoke. They shared their tears quietly and privately. Elsie watched her mother pack the last bundles for the trip. Her mother's sure and gentle hands moved slowly over the clean dresses and slips. These same hands had guided Elsie's own as she learned to weave baskets and braid her own hair.

Sadly, Elsie set aside her buckskin doll. She knew she could not take things that would make the nuns

By Roberta Haines

think of her Indian home. Her mother packed only a few blankets, clothing and food for the long trip: camas lily bulbs, dried and pounded into cakes, and chunks of dried fish and deer meat.

When Elsie and her mother finished packing, they went outside on the porch to wait in the warm, morning sunlight. Her uncle sat on the porch whittling. Elsie peered over her uncle's shoulder. "What are you making, Uncle?" she asked.

"This is a whistle made of willow," Uncle Twin-Star replied. "Your little sister will enjoy it. She can play it when she gets lonesome for you." He glanced at Elsie teasingly, "*If* she gets lonesome for you. She still remembers the time you wouldn't let her go riding with you, and the time you told her she couldn't jump off the cliff to swim."

The shavings from the whistle fell softly to the ground, near the parfleche (par-FLETCH), his rawhide pack.

Uncle Twin-Star, her mother's brother, was one of Elsie's favorite people. He was a gentle, quiet man who loved to laugh. Now, aware of their sadness, he teased Elsie and her mother just enough to make them smile. Hearing the affection in his voice, Elsie felt a little better, too. She loved his deep, easy chuckle and the way he listened.

He put his arm around Elsie and gave her a little squeeze. She saw the warm twinkle in his eyes and giggled in spite of herself. Uncle Twin-Star always talked to Elsie as if she were an important person in the tribe, not just a girl of ten years. He seemed to know things no one else knew. Now he looked up at Elsie and asked, "Are you ready?"

"Yes," whispered Elsie, but she didn't feel ready.

18

She looked down at her feet—at the soft foot covering of her moccasins. Soon she would be wearing hard, ugly shoes from the mission. Last year she had been given a pair that were too small. Suddenly, tears caught in her throat again and burned her eyes. She tried not to let her uncle see them.

Uncle Twin-Star put his knife and carving in his parfleche, patting the porch next to him, inviting Elsie to sit. He looked at her with soft, shining eyes. She sat down.

"Elsie, do you remember old Wolf, your grandpa's dog?"

Elsie nodded. "I was six when Wolf left our tribe. He was old and just never came back." But she remembered the warmth of his big, furry body. He had been nearly as tall as she. They had played together. Wolf was much stronger than Elsie, but he was always gentle. She remembered riding on his powerful back, her hands full of his fur, when she was very small. She had leaned on his shoulders, pulled his tail and followed him everywhere.

"When you were about four years old," Uncle Twin-Star said, "your mother was picking berries on our berrying ground. You wandered into the grazing area of Mr. Frank's old bull. The bull charged. You were all alone. Your mother was too far away to help. But Wolf flew across that meadow. He ran between you and the bull, drawing the bull away."

"Then I wasn't alone," said Elsie, "because of Wolf."

Her uncle smiled at her. He stood up and put his hand on her shoulder. "Such times as these are filled with power, Elsie. Think on this and remember we can learn from everything around us: our family, our people, each tree, every animal, and even the songs of the water and wind.

"The government wagon comes for you. It's okay. You can learn from the missionaries, too. So you will know that you are not alone, I have told you your story. It is your gift and your lesson from home this year. And to help you remember what Wolf has to teach you, I have brought you something more." From the pack at his feet, her uncle pulled out a wooden horse.

Elsie took the horse in her hands. She stroked its smooth, curved neck. The horse's short mane reminded her of Wolf's thick fur. "Did you make this, Uncle?"

Uncle Twin-Star's eyes twinkled. "I know the mission school will not let you keep an Indian toy. But I wanted you to have something from your home.

"I have thought on this, Elsie. It is important that we, your people, be with you on this long journey. I have been watching for the thing that will help my niece remember we are always with her.

"At the fishing grounds this year, a young suiyape (su-ee-YAH-pay) American was there with Spokane James. He was traveling to Yakima. Their wagon wheel broke, spilling a trunk onto the road. This horse fell out, landing almost at my feet. When the wheel was fixed, I asked the suijape about the horse. He said it was his own as a boy. We spoke of you and the mission school. He admired my tobacco pouch. We talked more. And so it goes. A little horse has arrived among the Wenatchi-pum (wen-AH-chee-pum) to go to the mission school with Elsie."

Elsie hugged her uncle hard. She felt his warm, strong arms around her and the little horse. When the government wagon came, she clutched his gift and said a brave good-bye to her family.

Now, riding in the dusty wagon, it was hard to believe she had been home only yesterday. In one arm she

20

cradled the wooden horse. Her other arm comforted one of the youngest girls, who had cried herself to sleep. There were ten children in the wagon. Some of them had been very frightened when their mothers handed them into the wagon. The youngest ones had cried. Some had fought. Their mothers' eyes looking up at them were dark, glistening pools.

"It's okay. You'll be all right," each mother soothed in her own language. Wenatchi (wen-AH-chee), Methow (met-HOW), Chelan (SHAH-lan), Entiat (EN-tee-at), Okanogan (o-kan-AH-gann). "We'll be right here waiting for you. Go. I love you."

Elsie understood all five languages. But at the school, she was allowed to speak only English.

The government men driving the wagon did not talk to the children. One held a rifle. The other held the reins. The long hard wagon ride seemed to last forever. When they arrived at the mission, Elsie was so tired she was almost glad to be there. Almost, but not quite. She still remembered her first year at the mission. It had been bad. She had been punished many times for speaking her own language. But this year was her third. She thought she could remember enough English.

The nuns in their long, black habits put the children in lines. They asked for their names and ages. Then, the children and their belongings were taken to the laundry room. The nuns thought they were unclean. When they were thoroughly washed and dressed in different clothing, the children gathered in lines outside the dining room. Here they began to learn about the mission prayers. Elsie remembered most of the words. But the children who had not been to the mission before stood in mute confusion. After the meal, Elsie and the others were marched to the dormitories.

"It's just the same," thought Elsie, her heart sinking as she entered the dormitory. Rows of beds lined the long, bare room. Each girl was assigned to a bed. Their belongings were kept in a closet in another room. A laundry bag for dirty clothing hung at the end of each bed. After the nuns led them in prayers, Elsie and the other children climbed wearily into bed. The lamps were put out.

Elsie lay awake. She could hear the smothered sobs of another child several beds away. The hard, cold sheets felt scratchy and strange. She missed her mother and father and the warmth of her home. She missed her uncle, and Wolf. She thought about her uncle's story. Suddenly, she remembered the wooden horse.

"Where is it?" she thought, frightened. The horse was not on her bed. She knew the rules. No one was to get out of bed after "lights-out." But she had to find her uncle's gift. Elsie sat up cautiously. The bedsprings creaked and groaned beneath her. She froze, listening. The bed beside hers made a brief racket as a girl turned over in her sleep.

"I'll get up fast," decided Elsie, "maybe they won't notice." She slid out of bed quickly and hurried down the dark, cold hall.

The closet. The horse had to be there. She slipped around the corner and tugged open the door. It was so dark that she couldn't see a thing. Elsie felt panicky. What if someone found her? She took a deep breath and whispered her own prayer in her own language. The words made her feel calm and strong. She began to search carefully through the clothes.

Elsie moved her hands over every shelf. Then she felt in every corner. Then between each layer of clothing. The horse was not there. Had one of the nuns taken it?

22

Or another child?

"Oh, dear Uncle Twin-Star," she thought, "I have lost your gift on the very first day." Aching with loneliness, she returned to her bed.

As she passed the foot of her bed, she brushed against the laundry bag. It swung free and settled back into place with a soft thump. Something was inside. Something too heavy to be clothing. Elsie bent down and felt inside the bag. Her fingers touched polished wood. There!

Holding the wooden horse close to her, she climbed back into bed. Suddenly, she had the powerful feeling that her whole family stood around her. Her heart seemed to sing with their love. She thought about her uncle's words: "So you will know you are not alone, I have told you your story."

Her uncle was right. She was not alone.

 *I stayed with Elsie for many years. She put me on the front counter in the store she and her husband ran. I watched all the people who came in and out. One day a young Black man in an Army uniform came in. He grinned at me and said I was just the right gift for his younger brother. . . .*

3

1910's

Missing Friends
Albert's Story

Albert sat on the front porch after school, waiting for his dad to come home from the mine. On the step beside him stood a little wooden horse.

"I am bored," Albert told his horse. As usual, nothing much was happening in Roslyn. A dog walked along the unpaved street, stopping to sniff at each white picket fence. Inside the house, Albert could hear his sisters giggling.

"They're no fun," he told Horse. "They never want to play baseball or go fishing." Albert sighed. He hadn't been fishing since Sam joined the Army.

Horse had been a gift from his older brother Sam. Two days later, Sam's unit of Black soldiers[1] had been sent off to the war in France.

Albert missed his brother a lot. And it seemed like everyone who was any fun had moved away. His friend Bobby Gianelli (GEE-ann-el-ee) had moved so his dad could find work at the mine in Newcastle. And now, Anthony Cirone (sir-OWN) had moved to Black Diamond.

By Esther Mumford

"He was teaching me Italian," Albert told Horse. "Now I don't have any friends, except you."

He heard voices coming down the street. It was the miners, on their way home from work. He saw his dad among the tired crowd. He was covered with coal dust. All of the miners, black and white, were dark with coal.

His dad turned toward the house. He wore dark blue coveralls, rubber boots and a miner's cap. On the miner's cap was the small lamp he used inside the mine. He grinned at Albert.

"Hey, Albert," called his dad. "Why are you looking so down in the mouth?"

"I dunno," said Albert glumly.

"Missing your friend?" asked his dad. "Tell you what. If you meet me at the mine tomorrow after work, I'll take you fishing."

Albert hugged his dad, despite the coal dust. "Hooray, hooray, hooray!" he said. He always said things three times when he was excited.

"You bring the poles and bait," said his dad. Then, still smiling, he pointed at the coal smudges on Albert's shirt. "Now we'll both have to wash for supper."

At supper, the whole family gathered around the table. Everyone was quiet while Dad said grace. Albert looked across the table at his brother's empty chair. He sure missed Sam. He added a special prayer, asking God to take good care of Sam. "Amen," said everybody.

His sisters started talking right away. Albert found it hard to get a word in until Louise and Emma both had mouthfuls of ham and collard greens.

"Mother," he asked. "Can I take Sam's picture to school tomorrow? We're going to talk about the war. Miss Brown said we could bring something to share."

"All right, Albert," said his mother. "If you promise

to be very careful. And bring the photograph to Mrs. Benedetti's (ben-i-DEE-tee) right after school."

In school the next day, Miss Brown showed the class a map of France. Albert showed everyone Sam's picture. His brother wore a uniform and cap.

"Sam is in the Army," he said proudly. "He and the other Black soldiers in his unit dig trenches and latrines for the United States. Sam says that some other Black Americans are soldiers for France. They don't dig trenches or latrines. He sent me a postcard with French words on it. But I don't know how to speak French."

"Thank you, Albert," said Miss Brown. "Who else has brothers in the Army?" Hands shot up all around the room. Albert went back to his seat. He sure missed Anthony. Any time one of them had to make a speech in class, the other one used to look at his friend, wink and give a thumbs up sign.

After school, he took Sam's picture to Mrs. Benedetti's. His mother and the other Roslyn women, black and white, had gathered to knit socks for the soldiers in France. Emma and Louise were there, too.

"Some new people moved in next door today," said Emma.

"While we were at school," added Louise.

Albert didn't care. He was in a hurry to go fishing. But as he ran home to get the poles, he wondered if the new family would have a boy his age. When Bobby Gianelli had lived on the corner, two houses away, they had walked to school together every day.

At home, he put down his lunch bucket, and gathered up his knapsack, the bamboo fishing poles and a can of worms.

"Come on, Horse," he said. He stuffed the wooden horse into his knapsack. "We're going fishing! Look out crappies, here we come!" Carrying the fishing gear, Albert headed down to the mine to meet his dad.

As he rounded the corner, near the mine, Albert could see the double tracks leading into the dark entrance of the mine. Inside the mine, mules pulled the ore-cars filled with coal. The tracks brought the ore-cars and the man-cars carrying the miners to the surface. He saw the pulleys near the tracks begin to vibrate.

A moment later, the man-cars, looking like boxes on wheels with doors at each end, came to the top of the slope and stopped near where he was standing. He scanned the ten soot-stained faces in the first car. Then he scanned the second car, where he spotted his dad, who waved and grinned at him.

"Can we go to Ronald?" he asked as soon as his dad climbed down from the man-car. "That's where the fishing is best, best, best!" Albert also liked the stories his dad told about living in Ronald when he was a boy.

Albert thought about the stories as they started down the trail. His grandparents had come to Ronald a long time ago, before Washington was even a state. The Roslyn mine had opened a few years earlier. There was almost nothing in Ronald then, just the mine and a few houses. The Black people who came to Ronald built a church. They hired a teacher to teach the miners' children.

They had classes in the church, thought Albert, because they didn't have a school. A low branch slapped across his face.

"Ouch," said Albert. He decided he had better pay attention to the trail. In June, all the trees had leaves. Some of the branches hung heavy and low across the trail. He ducked another branch. It was cool and dark in the woods. Ahead he could see his dad, moving through the shadows. A third branch grabbed at his cap. Albert took his cap back and hurried to catch up with his dad. He was glad he wasn't alone in the woods.

Pretty soon they came to the stream near Ronald. Albert's dad baited the hooks. Albert liked fishing, but he didn't like putting the worm on the hook.

Before long, Albert felt a tug on his line. He pulled a crappie out of the water. Then his dad caught a perch. Albert looked out over the water. This was one of his favorite places. He liked the way the sun felt on his face and the way it glinted on the water. He liked the quietness too. I wish I could do this every day, he thought. They fished until Albert had caught five fish and his dad had seven.

"Well," said his dad, "let's leave some for next time. Your mother will be wanting to start supper." They cleaned the fish and headed home through the woods.

It was darker now under the tall trees. Dodging branches, Albert hurried up the trail, close behind his dad. He didn't want to get lost in the woods. Anthony Cirone had gotten lost one time, and stayed out almost all night! The thought of it made Albert shiver.

He let out a sigh of relief when he saw the lights of Roslyn and the outline of houses along the streets. They turned onto their own street. Albert caught a whiff of flowers. At home, there was a welcoming lamp burning in the front window. Albert and his dad went around to the back to draw water. They washed up before they went inside.

His mother and sisters were in the kitchen, peeling potatoes and chopping onions and tomatoes from his mother's garden.

"Goodness," said his mother when she saw the fish. "I don't think we can eat all these. Albert, take some of these fish over to the people next door." She was grinning at him like there was some kind of joke. He looked around the kitchen. Emma and Louise were smiling, too. Puzzled, Albert went outside.

He climbed the steps of the house next door and knocked. A boy who was about his own height and size opened the door. It was Bobby Gianelli!

"Oh boy, oh boy, oh boy!" said Albert. He and Bobby hugged one another and jumped up and down. Their caps fell off. Bobby picked up Albert's and Albert picked up Bobby's. They looked at each other and started laughing. Mrs. Gianelli came to the door to see what all the noise was about.

"Oh, it's you, Albert," she said, smiling. "Your mother promised not to spoil the surprise. Won't you come in?"

"Yes, ma'am," said Albert. "My mother sent me to bring these fish to you for your supper."

"That's very kind," said Mrs. Gianelli. "I haven't had time to cook, what with all these boxes." Albert could see moving boxes stacked against the walls. Mr. Gianelli appeared from the other room. He looked tired.

"Hello, Albert," he said, "good to see you again."

"Welcome back, sir." Albert looked over at Bobby and grinned. He sure was glad to see Bobby!

Soon, Albert's mother called him home for supper. After supper, Albert did his homework and went next door where his father was talking to Mr. Gianelli about work at the mine. Bobby and Albert were full of plans.

After he went home, Albert helped his sisters with the dishes. Then it was time for bed. Albert carried Horse upstairs with him. When his mother blew out the lamp, he snuggled happily under the covers.

"Good night, Horse," he whispered. "You and me

have got a friend!" Thinking about all the fish he and Bobby Gianelli would catch together, he fell asleep.

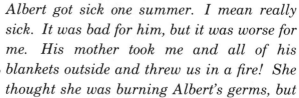 *Albert got sick one summer. I mean really sick. It was bad for him, but it was worse for me. His mother took me and all of his blankets outside and threw us in a fire! She thought she was burning Albert's germs, but instead she burned me! When things cooled down, I found myself lying in a pile of ashes. . . .*

NOTE: The term "Negro" was commonly used to describe Afro-Americans in the early 1900's. However, we have chosen to use "Black" because it is more familiar today. The term "Black" was used historically as well. Newspapers of the late 1800's spoke of "Black miners." The train carrying these miners was called the "Black Train."

4

1920's

The Footlog
Henry's Story

School had been out a couple of weeks and it was boring around home. My best friend was visiting his grandmother in Seattle. I sat in the living room, just staring out the window. Across the room, Mom was working at the town's telephone switchboard. I listened to the phone lines buzzing and tried to think of something to do.

There isn't much to do in Darrington. I mean, no movies or swimming pool or skating rink. I don't even have a bike. I like fishing and hiking in the woods, but Mom doesn't like me to go alone. She's afraid I'll come across some high place and freeze up.

You see, I have this awful fear of heights. A phobia, my mom calls it. She says it's nothing to be ashamed of, but I hate it. If my friends ever find out they'll call me a coward.

In between calls Mom kept looking at me, like she was worried. "Is something bothering you, ba—Henry?"

She knows I hate it when she calls me "baby." After all, I'm nearly twelve. But since last year she's been acting like a worried hen.

By Kathryn Armstrong

"No. There's just nothing to do around here."

Mom got a sad look on her face, like she was going to cry. "If your father was alive. . . . "

"It's okay, Mom. Never mind."

I miss my dad too, but I guess it's worse for her. He was killed up at Sauk (SOK) lumber camp last year. He was a faller. When his partner yelled "Timber!" he jumped out of the way, but the tree split, kicked back and hit him.

Now my mom has to work. She got this job running the town telephone office. She says we're lucky that she has a job because there aren't many places for women to work. But I don't feel so lucky. These days she babies me something awful.

Mom had her head turned away, but I could tell she was crying. Then a call came in on the long distance line. She cleared her throat and sniffed a little bit before she put the plug in. "Darrington," she said into the mouthpiece.

Then she smiled, right through the tears on her face. "That's wonderful," she said. "Henry will be so happy."

"Happy about what?" I asked. "Who are you talking to?"

Mom held one hand up and hushed me, but she was still smiling. "Okay dear," she said into the phone. "We'll see you tomorrow."

She pulled out the plug and turned to me. "Your Uncle Harold is coming on the stage tomorrow. He was laid off at the coal mine. He may stay with us for a while."

Well, that was good news. I like Uncle Harold a lot. He's been working in Roslyn in a coal mine. Mom worries about him, too. He's Mom's younger brother and I think she likes to baby him like she does me.

I went uptown the next day to meet the stage. I was

34

early so I bought a Baby Ruth candy bar for a nickel. Then I hung around in front of the pool hall and peeked in. Mom would skin me alive if I ever went inside.

Uncle Harold was the first one off the stage. He hugged me so hard he nearly broke my ribs. I felt happier than I had for a long time.

We had a good time that night, sitting around listening to Uncle Harold's mining stories. Then he said, "I'm going to try to get on up at Sauk Camp."

Mom had a fit!

"Please don't, Harold. It's so dangerous! You must know. . . . "

"I know how you feel, Sis. Don't worry so much. I'll be just fine." Seeing she was still doubtful, he stood up with a grin. "Wait 'till you see what I found the other day."

He went to his suitcase and pulled out a little wooden horse. "I found this little beauty in a pile of ashes near the mine. He must have been burned when some poor kid was quarantined with scarlet fever. He's in pretty bad shape, but I'm going to make him good as new."

I couldn't see what was so great about an old toy horse. But Uncle Harold acted like it was some kind of treasure.

"I'll whittle some new legs for him at night in the bunkhouse. If I get a job, that is."

Mom didn't say anything, but she still looked unhappy. He went up to the camp the next morning. They hired him right away. I was tickled because I knew I'd see him every week.

When Uncle Harold came down from camp the next week, he asked Mom if I could go up to the camp for a day. "I think he'd enjoy seeing what a logging camp looks like," he said. "There's a great fishing spot not far from where I'm bucking logs. It's only a short distance. You won't have to worry about him, Sis."

I didn't think Mom would ever say yes. But Uncle Harold coaxed until she finally gave in.

On Monday morning I got up at five o'clock. I was too excited to eat much breakfast. We went up to the depot and climbed on the big speeder with all the loggers. They were real friendly. Some of them gave me pointers about fishing.

The long ride up to the camp was fun—except for one part. A couple of times we went over high trestles above the river. I made the mistake of looking down the first time. When I saw the Sauk River swirling and rushing way down below, I nearly panicked. I was scared to death, but I couldn't look away. I just stood there and shook. Uncle Harold took my arm and slowly turned me around and helped me sit down.

Uncle Harold understands about my phobia. He never teases me about it or calls me a coward. That's one of the things I love about him.

The rest of the ride was fun after I got over being scared. The Tarheel loggers were sure funny. They came out here from North Carolina. They told jokes and smoked tobacco until the air was so thick I nearly choked. But their jokes were so funny that I had to keep laughing.

When we got to the camp, Uncle Harold told me to look around while he went to the cookhouse to get our lunch. There were five or six bunkhouses. I peeked inside one and saw double rows of bunks on each side. There was a big heating stove made out of a barrel in the middle of the room.

Near the cookhouse was the office. It was like a small store with candy, tobacco, fishing supplies, magazines and a few clothes. The bookkeeper sat in a little room at one end. I bought a jar of salmon eggs. Then Uncle Harold stuck his head in the door. "Ready to go, kid?"

He had a lunch pail and his bucking saw and a bottle of kerosene for oiling it. He looked happy. "This sure beats coal mining, Henry," he said as we started out. "It's a whole lot cleaner, too." I carried the lunch pail and my fishing pole. We set off through the woods, walking fast.

In about twenty minutes we came to the clearing where the logs were. Uncle Harold oiled his saw and got right to work. I watched him for a few minutes. The saw cut quickly through the big logs. Pretty soon he was sweating. He stopped sawing and stripped down to his undershirt.

"Where's the fishing hole, Uncle Harold?" I asked.

He pulled out a big handkerchief and mopped his face. "See that trail right over there? Just follow that and you'll come to a creek. You go across and follow the trail a half mile or so until you come to a smaller creek. That's where the big ones are. Find a spot below a riffle or under an overhanging bank, and you'll get your limit in no time. Good luck, kid."

I started out, feeling really good, until I reached the creek. Then I saw it! A footlog! It was about fifteen feet above the creek and really narrow. No way! I thought. I looked downstream and upstream. The only other way to get across was to wade and that was impossible. The steep bank down to the edge was covered with nettles. And anyway, the water was too deep and swift.

Finally, after standing there shaking in my boots for what seemed like an hour, I got down on my hands and knees. Holding onto my fishing pole with a death grip, I began inching my way across. I was trembling and almost crying. I tried not to look down at the rushing water, but I couldn't help it. I've never been so scared!

Why hadn't Uncle Harold told me about the log? Was he trying to test me? I sure was glad he wasn't there to see me, crawling along an inch at a time.

Finally I made it across. I was too weak to stand up for a couple of minutes. But I was happy to be on the other side!

When I felt better I hurried on to the other creek, trying not to think about the return trip. Pretty soon I came to the smaller creek.

Uncle Harold was right about the fishing hole. As soon as I had my line in the water I felt a tug. I pulled in a big, shiny trout! This was great! I baited my hook again and two minutes later I got another one.

I was pulling in my third fish when I heard a shout. "Henry! That's a beaut!"

It was Dr. Blair. He was fishing downstream. I put the fish on the notched stick with the others and held them up. He waved his pole and smiled, then cast his line again. I fished for a while longer and then I suddenly realized I was starving. I yelled goodbye to the doctor and started back down the trail. As I got closer to that log I decided I wasn't so terribly hungry after all. All I was, was scared! Holding my rod high above my head, I started off upstream through the brush. I figured the creek would be smaller, the farther I went. In about ten minutes I found a place where I could wade across. The water was freezing cold, but I didn't care.

By the time I got back to the clearing I had nettle stings, cold wet feet, and an empty stomach. At first I didn't see Uncle Harold. Then I heard a moan.

I looked behind the big log he'd been cutting. The saw was still in the log, halfway through. Uncle Harold lay on the ground, a big branch beside him. Blood was streaming from a gash on his head. His hair was matted with it and his face was covered with blood, too.

I saw right away what had happened. It was what they call a widow maker. A loose limb had blown out of a tree and sideswiped his head. I knew he wasn't dead, but he looked pretty bad. I had to get help! It was a long walk back to the camp. Then I remembered Dr. Blair.

I started to run, faster than I ever had in my life. But when I saw the footlog, I froze in my tracks. Then I thought about Uncle Harold's bloody face. I had to get to Dr. Blair in a hurry! Without looking down, I walked steadily across. On the other side, I started running again. "Dr. Blair, Dr. Blair!" I yelled when I saw him. He dropped his pole and ran toward me. Going back, it was even easier to cross the log. I was worried about Uncle Harold, but at the same time I felt good inside.

Uncle Harold had to have stitches and he was laid off work for a couple of days. He hated being laid up.

"You need something to do," I told him. "How about fixing that old horse?"

He made new legs that move back and forth. When he was finished, Uncle Harold gave the horse to me. I let Mom put it up on the piano. She's crazy about that horse. I'd rather have a new Columbia bike. But for now, I'm going fishing. And if I come to a footlog, I know I'll be able to cross it.

 *When Henry was older, he and his mother moved to Seattle. They took me along. But I don't think Henry ever liked me all that much. One day he put me in a box and carried me upstairs. And I sat there in the dark.* Just sat there! *I thought nothing exciting would ever happen again . . .*

5

1930's

The Mysterious Delaneys
Katy's Story

"There he is, Watson." Katy lifted her wooden horse onto her bedroom window sill so he could see. "There's that strange Delaney boy. He's so mysterious."

Katy liked mysteries. She liked to pretend she was Sherlock Holmes, the famous detective. She had named her horse after Dr. Watson, Sherlock's friend. A mystery surrounded Watson, too. She had found him in her aunt's attic in Seattle almost a year ago, just before they moved to Mason City. But Aunt Wilma couldn't tell Katy anything about where the horse came from.

Katy looked out the window again. Ralph Delaney was walking past her friend Babette's house now. "I'll look for clues at school today," she promised Watson.

"Hurry up, Katy!" Mama called. "You'll be late for school." Katy's brother, Clay, had already left. Katy put Watson back on the shelf, gave her mother a kiss and ran out the door. She trotted down the street to Babette's house, her brown braids bouncing on her back.

"I'm going to solve a mystery," she told Babette as they walked to school. "You can help."

"What mystery?" asked Babette.

By Judy Laik

"The Delaneys. They're so unfriendly. When I say 'hi' to Ralph, he always turns away."

"Maybe he's shy," Babette said. "They just moved here."

Katy shook her head. She didn't think so. All the families of the workers building Grand Coulee Dam were friendly with each other—except the Delaneys. Maybe they had something to hide.

At recess, Katy walked around the school yard until she spotted Ralph Delaney. She watched him carefully, looking for clues. He was reading a book. He paid no attention to the games being played around him. A ball escaped from the seven-up game Babette and Katy's other friends were playing, and bounced past Ralph. He jumped up like a startled animal. What is he afraid of? Katy wondered. She joined her friends' game. As she bounced the ball against the school wall, she thought of a way to find out.

After school, she told Babette her plan. "Let's go to the Delaneys' tonight and look in their window."

"We can't do that!" Babette protested.

"Why not? I want to see what they're doing. They're a mystery, and I intend to solve it."

"But you can't spy on people. It's... it's probably illegal."

"Maybe the Delaneys are doing something illegal. They sure act like it. If you won't come, I'll go by myself."

Babette shuddered. "Oh, Katy. But my parents won't let me stay out late at night."

"It wouldn't be late. It's dark by seven. We could do our homework at the library and then stop by the Delaneys' on our way home. It would only take a few minutes."

"Well, all right," said Babette.

In the dark that night, after going to the library, Katy and Babette stealthily approached the Delaneys' house. Katy clutched Watson. "This is it, Watson," she whispered excitedly to the horse.

"Katy?" Babette sounded nervous.

"Shh." Quietly they crept up to the Delaneys' house. Babette gave Katy a boost up to the window. Holding Watson in one hand, Katy looked inside.

Mr. Delaney sat in a chair reading the newspaper. Ralph was doing homework at the table, and Mrs. Delaney was sewing a dress. Through the glass Katy could hear a radio playing. Her heart sank. Everything looked so ordinary.

She looked around the brightly lit room, searching for clues. Nothing seemed strange or out of place. But wait a minute! She looked again at the half-finished dress. It was far too small for Ralph's mother. "What do you think, Watson?" she whispered to the horse.

Suddenly, Babette sneezed and let go of Katy. Katy's head bumped the window. Her elbow cracked against the sill. Pain shot up her arm, and she gave a muffled shriek. As she crashed to the ground, she heard a little girl's voice inside the house.

Katy and Babette ran. Behind them, Mr. Delaney shouted from his doorway, "Who's there? Come back! I'll call the police!"

Katy and Babette held a whispered conference on Katy's porch. Watson listened.

"There's a girl in that house," said Katy.

"It was Ralph you heard," Babette countered.

"I'll prove it to you," Katy said, her curiosity growing. Why would the Delaneys pretend there were only three of them?

At school the next day, she confronted Ralph. He

looked up from his book, his eyes wary. "Who's that girl in your house?" she demanded.

Ralph turned pale. "It's Marie. Sh-she's my sister."

"Your sister? Then why do you hide her?"

Ralph glared at her like he wished she would disappear. Katy waited. Finally he said, "She's crippled. People stare at her. She hates it, so she stays in the house."

"Oh," said Katy, then added, "isn't she lonely?" And bored, she thought. How awful—to stay inside all the time!

"I guess so." He looked sad and then angry. "Look, why don't you just go away?"

"Wait a minute," Katy said. She had a new plan. President Roosevelt was coming to Mason City in a few days to see the dam. He had been crippled, too.

"Could I come and see Marie?" She asked.

Ralph looked at her, his face puzzled. "I don't know. I'll have to ask her."

The next day, for Katy's tenth birthday, her father said she could come and watch him work.

Katy liked watching the work on the dam. It wasn't mysterious, but it was exciting. Huge earth-moving machines had dug an enormous hole in the Columbia River channel. Katy's father was one of many carpenters building forms to pour concrete into. After the concrete hardened, the forms would be torn down. Katy told Watson how big the dam would be.

"It will hold back the whole river," she said. "The Grand Coulee Dam will generate electric power, and store water to irrigate the desert for miles around."

After she got home, Ralph came to the front door of her house. "Marie says you can come," he announced. Carrying Watson, Katy ran to the Delaneys' house.

Marie lay on a sofa in the parlor, with a quilt over her legs. Her face was thin and very pale.

"Guess what, Marie?" Katy started talking right away. "When I was at the dam site today, Mr. Banks, the head boss, came up to me. He asked if he can borrow Watson. He has an Indian figure, and he wants him to sit on Watson on a model of the dam, just for the President's visit!"

Marie laughed, and her pale face brightened. "Who's Watson, and why does Mr. Banks want him to sit on a model of the dam?" she asked.

Katy showed her the horse. "It's to show President Roosevelt how big the dam will be," she explained. Soon the girls were talking like old friends. When Marie's mother came into the room, Katy saw the surprised, pleased look on her face. Now, she thought, nodding at Watson, it's time for my plan.

"Marie," she said. "Come and see the President with me!" Marie glanced over at her mother. Mrs. Delaney looked fearful.

"I don't know," she said. "People will stare. Someone might say something to hurt my Marie."

"President Roosevelt won't stare," said Katy. "He had polio, you know."

"Oh, Ma, can I? I want to go. Please!"

"Maybe," Mrs. Delaney said, "I'll have to ask your Pa."

While President Roosevelt addressed the Mason City people, Katy stood almost at the front of the crowd. Marie sat in her wheelchair beside Katy. The sun shone brightly. Mr. Banks stood by the model of the dam. The President finished speaking. Mr. Banks placed Watson, with the Indian figure sitting astride his back, on top of the model to show the relative size. Then, as the President's party started to leave for Mason City, Mr. Roosevelt stopped to talk with Marie. "What's your name?" he asked.

Blushing, Marie answered him. Gently, he asked what was wrong with her legs.

"They're twisted," she told him. "I need an operation."

"I see." President Roosevelt turned and whispered something to the man he was leaning on. As he walked stiffly the few steps to his limousine, Marie turned in her wheelchair to gaze after him. Her thin face glowed.

A few days later, when Katy went to visit her, Marie's face shone with excitement.

"Katy! Guess what? I'm going to Children's Orthopedic Hospital in Seattle. I'm going to have my operation! The President arranged it!"

"Oh, good!" Katy glanced down at Watson. She knew he must be proud. He had done more than help her solve a mystery. Soon Marie would be able to walk!

"I'll miss you, Katy," Marie said softly.

Impulsively, Katy thrust the horse into Marie's hands. "Take Watson with you," she said. "So you won't be lonely. I'll still have Babette to play with."

She would miss Marie, and Watson too. But she was glad Marie would be able to play outside when she came home again.

 *Marie gave me to another little girl when she left the hospital. I was disappointed. Solving mysteries with Katy had been fun. For a while I lived at the hospital. Then I was put into another box and taken to a second hand store. One day a little girl looked in the window....*

NOTE: Native Americans living near Grand Coulee Dam opposed its construction. The dam flooded 80,000 acres of reservation land. It destroyed fish runs and fishing places on the Columbia River. But, when the dam builders needed a figure for the scale model, they chose a Native American on a horse.

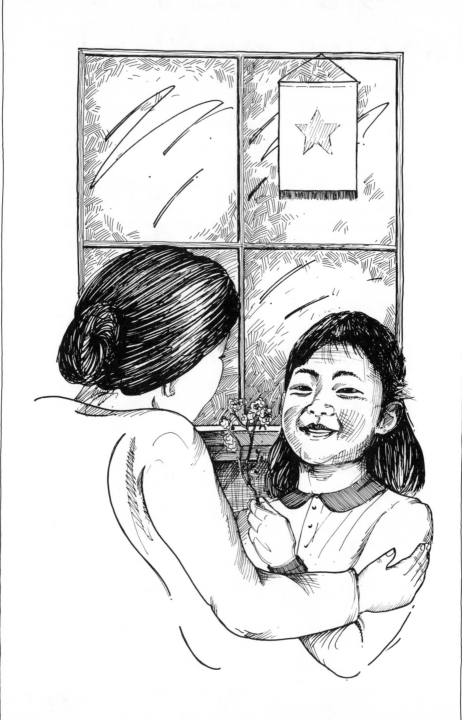

6

1940's

Not Much, But Enough
Mariko's Story

"Hey, Mari, want to play kick-the-can after lunch?"

Mariko (mah-REE-koh) Kubota (koo-BOH-tah) smiled at her brother, Tadao (tah-DOW). She shook her head, aware of one small spot of silence in the crowded mess hall. It held her attention more than the clatter of dishes and the mix of Japanese and English spoken all around her. Across the long table, beside a tiny white-haired woman, sat a girl her own age who said nothing at all.

"No, Tadao," she said, "I want to write to Barbara."

"Aw, you can write letters anytime," her brother protested.

"Maybe so," she agreed, "but here I can play anytime, too."

It's true, she thought. Ever since all of us Japanese were evacuated to this assembly center at the Puyallup (pew-ALL-up) Fairgrounds, there has been nothing else to do but play.

I never thought I'd get tired of it, but I do. All of us do. We get bored, and then we get crabby, even the grownups. They talk and talk, always asking the same

By Patricia Cochrane

49

questions. Where will they send us next? Will we have to wait until the war is over before we can go home?

They get angry and shout, she thought, because they are afraid. Then, being Japanese, we are all embarrassed. I wish someone would answer our questions. And I wish we could go home.

Mari missed her home on Vashon Island. And she missed her friend Barbara even more. Here she had no friends her age. She glanced across the table at the silent girl.

I wish we could be friends. But she won't even look at me. The girl's head was bowed low over her bowl. All Mari could see were her thick black bangs. She wondered if the other girl missed her friends, too. And school.

"Lucky you," Barbara had written. "On vacation already."

Mari chuckled softly. Poor Barbara, six more weeks of nouns and verbs and fractions. And poor me, six more weeks behind.

She risked another peek across the table. "Oh," Mari said, startled to see the girl's eyes meeting hers for the very first time. Mari smiled.

"I was wondering... " she began. She stopped when she saw the frown directed at her. The other girl looked down again.

"Please," Mari said. "Did I do something wrong?"

The girl jumped to her feet. She threw an angry look across the table and ran for the door.

"Wait!" Mari said. "What did I do?"

"Do not be offended by my granddaughter," said the tiny white-haired woman. "Yoshimi's (yoh-SHE-mee) father was taken away after the war began. He had a job with a Japanese firm. It seems he was even more of a

50

threat to the safety of this country than an old woman like me." She sighed and began to stack her dishes. "Then being sent to this camp... that was more than Yoshimi could bear. Since the day we arrived, she speaks to no one."

"I'm sorry," Mari said.

The old woman shook her head. "It is not your fault. Sad and hurtful things have happened to all of the people here."

Mari nodded. They had been forced from their homes with just the belongings they could carry. Everything else had been sold, stored or given away. And the worst thing was being interned just because they were Japanese, though many of them were nisei (NEE-say)—born here in Washington. All because the United States was at war with Japan.

"No trial, no guilt, just sent away," was what she'd heard her father say.

Back in the tiny room her family was assigned to, Mari flopped onto her cot and closed her eyes. She pictured Barbara doing the things they had done together until a month ago. Mari had lived on Vashon Island all her life. But how her life had changed! Even with her eyes closed she could hear and smell the changes.

She heard the swish of her mother's broom. She sneezed and opened her eyes. "Mama, you already swept this morning."

"Yes, Mariko-chan (mah-REE-koh-chann)," replied her mother. "And I will sweep again this afternoon. The mud becomes dust on our floor."

Mari laughed. "And you sweep it out to become mud again." Her laughter faded. Sweeping doesn't help the smell, she thought. Barbara didn't believe we are living in cow stalls, but it's true. What will she think of a girl

51

who won't talk? "Her grandmother is the only family Yoshimi has here," Mari wrote to Barbara. "I tried to make friends with her, but she ran away." She finished the letter and tucked it in her pocket.

Thinking of Barbara made her feel lonely. She picked up Far Strider, the little wooden horse she had brought from home. She had found him one day in a second-hand shop in Seattle. "I'm so glad I have you," she whispered. Deciding what to pack in the one suitcase she was allowed had been difficult. But Far Strider fit in her pocket, so there had been no question about leaving him behind. Mari smiled to think that now, without Barbara here, a wooden horse was her closest friend.

"I named you well, Far Strider. You came with me from Vashon Island to Puyallup. Where will you go next?" She slipped the horse into her pocket, too.

"Mama, I'm going to mail my letter," she said. Her mother looked up from her sweeping and nodded.

Mari ran out the door. As she cut around a corner of the long, shed-like building, she almost ran into someone. "Oops," she said, smiling in apology. Then she recognized Yoshimi. "Oh, it's you!"

Yoshimi frowned, but this time she didn't run away. Instead she thrust a piece of paper into Mari's hand. "What do you have to be happy about?" Mari read. She read it again. When she looked up, Yoshimi was gone.

All day Mari thought about Yoshimi's question. There were plenty of things to be unhappy about here: the starchy, unfamiliar food; the tiny room her family lived in; the guards and barbed wire fences; the sameness of each day.

Why am I happy then? she wondered. I didn't realize I was happy, but most of the time, I am. That night as she fell asleep, she was still puzzling over Yoshimi's question. In the morning she woke to the sound of Tadao whistling.

"What are you happy about? she asked curiously.

"Some people from town have sent bats and balls!" he said. "I'm going to join a team after breakfast. Want to come?"

"No," Mari said, thinking about Yoshimi's unanswered question. "I've got something to do."

Mari's father was dressed already and standing at the window. In the window hung a small white flag with a blue star.

"Look at this, Papa," Mari said, handing him Yoshimi's note. "How would you answer this question?" He read it, then touched the white flag. It meant that a member of their family—her brother Kobe (KOH-bee)—was in the United States Armed Forces.

"These flags hang proudly in homes all over America," he said quietly. "Pride brings happiness. There are twelve such flags in this camp, Mariko-chan. I am happy for all of them." He gave the note to his wife. She read it, then led Mari to the door. She pointed at the blossoms of a cherry tree outside the barbed wire fence.

"Look, Mariko-chan," she said. "The branches reach through the wire and right into this camp. Just as our friends back home keep reaching out to us in these difficult days. The blooming of the cherry tree gives me hope that this war will soon be over and we will go home again. That hope makes me happy." She went back inside.

Mari looked longingly at the cherry tree. She looked at the barbed wire fence running through its branches. It was forbidden to go near the fence. Armed guards patrolled the outside of the fence to make sure no one came near it.

Mari watched the guard march to the corner, then turn to walk back. When his back was to her, Mari took a slow step forward. Then, not stopping to think of what she was doing, or why, she ran to the fence, picked a tiny sprig and dashed back inside.

Mrs. Kubota snatched the flowers from Mari's hand and thrust them into her apron pocket. "Mariko," she gasped. "It is dangerous to go near the fence! How could you be so foolish?" She stared at her daughter for a long moment.

"Even so," she said, with a small smile, "the cherry blossoms bring hope to this barren place."

"Now," she said, pretending to be stern. "Go outside and play. I must sweep the floor."

Mari ran around the building and looked up the path. Yoshimi's grandmother walked toward her. She glanced at Mari and waved an envelope. "A letter," she cried happily. "From my son, Yoshimi's father. It is the first word from him since he was taken away." She gripped Mari's shoulder. Her hand shook with her excitement. "Will you find Yoshimi? She will read it to me."

Mari nodded. When she found Yoshimi she said, "Your grandmother wants you. I'll walk with you and answer your question. Come on." She led the way past the large muddy field the children called a playground.

A baseball game was in progress. Several adults stood along the baselines, coaching and encouraging the players in excited voices.

"People who care about what is happening to us sent those bats and balls," Mari said. "I'm happy about that."

Boldly, she grabbed Yoshimi's hand and ran with her to the window with the blue star. "I'm proud my brother is in the Army, serving America. Pride brings happiness."

54

She dropped Yoshimi's hand and said hesitantly, "These are things I'm happy about. They're not much, but they're enough for me." She smiled at Yoshimi. "Your grandmother has something to show you. Maybe it will make you happy too."

After that, Mari began to notice small changes in Yoshimi. Sometimes, in answer to a question, she would nod or shake her head. More than once Mari saw her smile at her grandmother. It wasn't much, Mari knew, but it was something.

Two months later, Mari was on a train, writing her weekly letter to Barbara. Tadao was playing checkers with their father. Her mother dozed in the corner of the seat.

June 22, 1942

Dear Barbara,

We're on our way to a permanent camp, but I don't know where yet. I'll send you my new address soon.

A sad thing happened to me today. In the confusion at the train depot I lost Far Strider. I haven't cried so hard since we left Vashon Island.

But a happy thing happened, too. Just before we left Puyallup, Yoshimi and her grandmother got a letter saying her father was being sent to the same camp. Yoshimi was so happy she talked to me for the first time!

Your friend,
Mari Kubota

Mari glanced out the window of the train. She smiled at her reflection in the dusty glass. In the seat behind her Yoshimi was chattering happily to her grandmother. It wasn't much, but it was enough.

 *When Mariko dropped me at the train station, all I could see were dozens of moving feet. I thought I would be trampled for sure. But somebody's foot kicked me into a dusty corner. I stayed there, watching trains and people come and go, until a fair-haired man dropped his hat right on top of me. . . .*

7

1950's

To Fish or Fly
Ole's Story

Ole (OL-ee) blinked as his brother Soren (SORE-en) switched on their bedroom lamp. "Ole, wake up. It's four o'clock. Time to go."

Ole Rolvaag (ROLL-vog) groaned. It was Saturday morning, the day of the big Boeing air show. Until last night, he had been excited about going to see the new planes and the model of the Sputnik with Soren and Uncle Jon. But at dinner Ole's father had ruined his plans.

"Lars is sick," his father said. "I'll need you on the boat tomorrow, Ole."

"But what about the air show?" Ole cried. "They're rolling out a mock-up of the 707! I can't miss that!"

"Sorry about that, Ole," said his father, his voice rolling like deep waves, "but the family business comes first. I need you on the boat."

After dinner, Ole appealed to Uncle Jon. "I really want to go with you!"

Uncle Jon shook his head. "Your dad needs you, Ole. It means a lot to him, having a son to follow in his footsteps."

Ole glanced across the room at his older brother.

By Tim Ryan

"Soren's lucky," he said. "I wish I wore a leg brace."

His uncle looked shocked. "Ole, you're the lucky one. You got the vaccination. Your brother had polio. That's nothing to wish for."

"But he gets to learn about science, and I have to fish!"

His uncle nodded. "I know it's hard for you. But your dad needs your help. He's a proud fisherman and sees a future in the sea."

Now, in the darkness before dawn on Saturday morning, Ole fretted that his dad needed him too much.

"I wish I was going with you, Soren."

"I know." His brother smiled sympathetically. "Fishing's hard work." As Ole pulled on his heavy clothes, Soren limped across the room and reached high on a shelf. Light from the bedside lamp reflected on his leg brace. He grabbed something out of the shadows beside his old hula-hoop trophy and put it in Ole's hand.

"For you, Ole."

"Your horse?" Uncle Jon had given Soren the little wooden horse when he first went out on his father's boat. "A survivor," their uncle said, explaining he had found the horse in a railroad station during the war. As long as Soren had gone out fishing, he kept the horse with him as a good-luck charm.

"It's yours now," Soren said quietly, pressing the horse into Ole's hand. "There's a peg in the cabin wall on dad's boat. That's where I always used to hang it."

At first, Ole felt pleased that his brother was giving him the horse. Then he wasn't sure. His family's expectations felt like a net he was caught in. They all want me to be a fisherman, he thought, as he and his father got into the car. Even Soren.

As they drove down to the Ballard waterfront, he

turned the horse restlessly between his hands. He still wished he was going to the air show.

The day promised to be mild and good for fishing. As Ole's father steered the boat out into Puget Sound, he was smiling. "Likely it'll be salmon and cod today," he said to Ole and Clem, the mate. He looked to the south and a small frown crossed his face like a cloud. "Might blow later, though."

Ole worked hard, winching in the nets and helping Clem empty the slippery fish into the hold. When the heavy nets were untangled, he helped Clem lead them out again. Sometimes Ole glanced overhead, hoping to spot an airplane. But mostly, he was too busy to think.

Later in the day, the Sound grew rough and a storm began to blow. Ole's father sent him below.

"Fishing's almost done," his father shouted over the wind. "Go on down where it's dry."

Ole struggled across the pitching deck to the cabin. Inside, he settled on his bunk. A queasy feeling lurched about in his stomach. This was the worst storm he had ever been in. When he peered outside, he saw white-capped waves rising all around the fishing boat. The wild motion of the waves made him feel worse. He shifted his gaze to the cabin walls. Soren had pasted up magazine photos of the planes their uncle worked on. On its peg near the door, the little wooden horse rocked side to side with the rolling of the boat.

"Why me?" he asked the horse. Ole wished achingly he had gone with Soren and Uncle Jon to the air show.

Suddenly he heard the wind-battered voice of his father. "Ole, Ole, come up on deck! The winch just broke!"

Ole pulled on his heavy gloves and scrambled up the hatchway. The boat bobbed and fell between wave crests, leaning first one way, then another. Ole steadied himself in the cabin doorway. Rain on the wind dashed across the deck, making everything wet and slippery. Taking a breath, he plunged out into the storm.

Ole's father pointed at the rail. "Grab hold, son. Help Clem pull that last net in!"

Ole staggered to the railing. Grabbing hold of the net, he began to pull. This was by far the worst storm he'd ever seen. He wished his father would hire another mate. Then he could build airplane models on Saturdays like Soren did.

Ole and Clem reached the end of the net, pulling a large tangled clump on deck.

"Good job, son!" his father bellowed from the bridge. "You too, Clem! Wouldn't you know? We get a little squall and the winch goes! Ole, you can go below now. I'll let you know if I need you, okay?"

Ole went back to the cabin, feeling miserable. I wish my father didn't need me, he thought. He pulled off his rain slicker and climbed wearily onto his bunk. The cabin was rocking more gently now and the wind had eased a little.

A few minutes later Clem came down to join him. "Don't worry, Ole," he said, brushing back his wet blond hair, "your Pop will run us in just fine. He's one of the best fishermen in Ballard. If anyone can run through a storm, it's him."

"I'm not worried," Ole said.

"Then what are you looking so glum about?" asked Clem.

"I just wish I had gone to the air show, that's all."

"What for?" wondered Clem. Ole stared at him, surprised by his lack of interest.

"To see the 707! That's the new four-jet plane my Uncle Jon is working on. And the model of the Sputnik!"

Clem leaned forward with a little more interest. "The satellite?" he asked. "The Russian satellite?"

"Yeah!" Ole felt excited, just thinking about it. The Sputnik was out in space right now, orbiting the earth.

"Say, Ole, I heard you could actually see that thing."

"When?" demanded Ole. "Really?"

"After sunset." Clem sat back, stroking his chin. "Now what did that guy say? If the light is just right and the satellite is passing from the dayside to the nightside."

"Maybe tonight, then," Ole said, and his heart soared, just like one of Uncle Jon's planes.

He waited impatiently for sunset. When the gray light faded, Ole jumped up from his bunk, whipping on his raingear. On the way out, he grabbed the wooden horse from his peg. Its old, curved lines felt comfortable in his hand.

"Come on, horse," he said. "We're going to look for the Sputnik!"

Thumb hooked between the horse's worn front legs, Ole sprang out on deck. He saw his father at the wheel, smiling in the glow of the bridge lights. The sea was still rough, but at the tattered edge of the sky, clouds rolled back to reveal stars.

Ole hurried over to the rail, staring up into the growing darkness. If the Sputnik came over, he'd be ready.

Gripping the rail and the horse, he waited. He scanned the sky, seeing only clouds and the unmoving stars. Disappointment grew inside him. Maybe the satellite would pass behind the clouds. Or maybe it would be too dim to see.

Suddenly something moved at the corner of his eye. He whirled around. And as he stared up at the point of light plowing straight and steady across the stars, Ole's heart flew.

63

The rail of the boat dipped in a heavy trough. Ole lurched and lost his balance. He grabbed the rail. As he did, he heard a faint splash. The horse! Ole leaned over the railing, staring down into the darkness. Soren's horse! The boat pitched again. He lost his grip and slid across the deck. In seconds, his father was there to grab him, shouting at Clem to take the helm. "Hold on, Ole. You almost lost it there! Don't give me scares like that!" His father lifted Ole to his feet and held him steady.

Heart pounding, Ole leaned against his father's arm. "Dad," he said. "I lost the horse. I lost Soren's horse!"

"That's your horse now, Ole."

"Yeah." He looked back at the sky, and his voice filled with air and wonder. "Dad," he said. "I saw the satellite."

"You saw the Sputnik?" His dad sounded uncertain. "You sure it wasn't just a shooting star?"

Ole smiled and shook his head. And although he felt sad about losing the horse, he knew his choice had been made the moment he saw the Sputnik.

He watched the night sky all the way to port. He had spotted the satellite and that knowledge filled him with excitement—something all the king salmon in the world couldn't do for him. It had been an electric moment, like the time Uncle Jon brought home their first television and crackling blue light filled the living room.

The nearer they got to shore, the more he brimmed with excitement at the thought of telling Soren and Uncle Jon he had seen the real Sputnik. And someday, he knew, he would fly.

 *Floating around in Puget Sound wasn't so bad. There were boats and birds and fish to look at. The tide carried me along. At last I washed up on a rocky beach. Then I got a little worried. The sand and rocks rubbed against me until I thought I would be worn away....*

8

1960's

Around The World's Fair
Julie's Story

"Look, Karen, there it is, there's the Space Needle!"
Julie cried. As her family rode the bus downtown, the
Space Needle, towering above the skyline, looked sharp
and new.

Today, thought Julie, I'll ride the elevator to the top
and look out at the world. All through the quiet summer
in Longview, Julie had been dreaming about this trip to
Century 21, the World's Fair. There would be exhibits
from countries all around the world, places she longed to
visit. "Look, Blanca," she whispered, holding her little
wooden horse up to the window. "Isn't it exciting?"

She had found Blanca, bleached white by saltwater,
on the beach one summer in Olympia. The little horse
looked old and she was sure it had traveled far. Now, on
her imaginary journeys, the little horse was always at
her side. Across the aisle of the bus, her father caught
her eye.

"Dreaming again?" he teased.

"Peter, don't," said her mother. "Imagination should
be encouraged." She looked seriously at her daughter.
"Now, Julie, dear, I'm counting on you to watch Karen.

By Mary Alice Sanguinetti

It's easy for a little girl to get lost at the fair."

Julie frowned. Why did she have to watch Karen? Her little sister was always interrupting her daydreams with questions.

They got off the bus at Westlake Mall near the monorail platform. The streets were bustling and cars roared past. Julie held Karen's hand tightly. She had never seen so many people. In her other hand she clutched Blanca.

A sleek white monorail train came gliding into the station. They stepped onto a "speed ramp" and moved effortlessly up to the train. Julie's father gave each girl a half dollar for her round trip fare. Then he slipped a couple of dollars into Julie's pocket. "For treats," he whispered.

"Thanks, Daddy," Julie whispered back. They all stepped onto the train and found seats. Julie and Karen pressed their faces against the window and gazed out at downtown Seattle. As the train zoomed silently toward the World's Fair, Karen leaned against her.

"Can I hold Blanca?" she asked. Karen was twisting one of her braids, like she always did when she was excited.

"Okay," said Julie. "But don't drop her."

They were quickly approaching the Space Needle. "95 seconds," announced Julie's father as the train slid into the station. The wonderful ride was over and they were among a throng of people descending from the train. Looking to see that her sister still had Blanca, Julie caught hold of Karen's hand.

"Where should we go first?" asked Julie's mother.

"The Food Circus!" said Karen. Julie pictured a tent full of performing hot dogs and giggled.

"No," she said, "the International Mall."

"How about the World of Science?" suggested Julie's father.

Julie's mother consulted the schedule of events. "There is a fashion show at the Interiors, Fashion and Commerce Pavilion."

"No, let's go to Science." Julie quickly sided with her father. She didn't want to look at clothes.

"We'll have time for the Food Circus and the International Mall, too," said her mother. "Julie, no wandering off now. And make sure you hold onto Karen's hand."

The World of Science started with a film explaining how scientists work. "They record what they see, and share what they've learned with other scientists," her father told them. Julie wished he would stop talking. She was on Darwin's ship, the H.M.S. Beagle, sailing toward Galapagos. She saw giant turtles and flightless birds and unfamiliar stars.

"Julie," Karen's voice broke through her daydream. "What's that man doing?" Reluctantly, she followed her parents and sister toward the next exhibit. In the small laboratory sat a scientist, surrounded by bottles of flies.

"Studying fruit flies," said Julie. "Yuck!"

"This way," said her father. They entered an auditorium and sat down. Overhead was a domed, white ceiling.

"This is Spacearium Central Control," announced a loud voice. "Prepare for takeoff." The auditorium faded into darkness.

"Julie, are we really going into space?" asked Karen.

"Shhh." Around her stars were blossoming. She saw the earth below, a misty blue and white ball, as they moved deeper into space. She was in a silver space ship, speeding through the vast darkness toward a tiny red speck. She was on the first American expedition to

Mars. When the lights came on again, she blinked and sighed.

"The Boeing Company helped sponsor this exhibit," Julie's father said as they left the auditorium, "and the projector they used has the world's largest wide-angle lens." Julie sighed again. She didn't want to know how everything worked. It spoiled the magic.

"I'm hungry," said Karen, as they passed the Food Circus.

"We'll eat later," said her mother. "Let's go to the Boulevards of the World." As they walked toward the Boulevards, Julie saw the Skyride ahead.

The Boulevards were lined with rows of shops. They surrounded a green rectangle of lawn and the International Fountain. Through the crowd, Julie caught a glimpse of the fountain; colored water sprayed from a dome in the middle of a huge concrete saucer. Her mother led them toward a shop on Boulevard West filled with Swiss clocks.

Julie looked around at all of the clocks. She liked the sound they made, all ticking at once with different voices. What would it be like to be a clockmaker? She imagined living in a small village in Switzerland. In the evening she would ride Blanca out of the village to watch the sun set over the Alps. Looking down to share this with Blanca, she realized that Karen was no longer beside her.

"Karen," Julie whispered, hoping her mother wouldn't notice. "Karen?" She darted out into the crowd, looking for her sister—past Mexican hats, past furniture from Hong Kong, past perfume from France. She saw the Skyride cars passing overhead. The shops and throngs of people blurred around her. Where was Karen? What would her mother say? She had to find her!

70

Up ahead she saw a hot dog stand. Maybe Karen was looking for something to eat.

Her heart pounding, Julie squeezed through the crowd. Delicious smells drifted toward her: pizza and fresh-baked pie. But she didn't feel hungry. Where, oh, where was Karen?

She pushed her way past a German restaurant and a man eating Belgian waffles. Finally she spied her sister's red sailor dress through the crowd. "Karen!" she shouted. "Over here. Karen!" Her sister turned around. There was a frightened look on her face.

"Karen, I'm so glad I found you," said Julie breathlessly.

Karen looked even more frightened. "Julie," she said. "Julie, I lost Blanca. I've been looking for her everywhere."

Julie's heart sank. How would they ever find a little horse among all these people? "It's okay," she lied. "We'll find Blanca later. Right now, we have to find Mommy."

"Don't you know where Mommy is?" Tears welled up in her little sister's eyes.

"Of course I do, silly," said Julie. "She's looking at Swiss clocks." Taking Karen's hand, Julie led the way around the fountain.

When they got back to the shop, it was filled with dolls instead of clocks. I can't let Karen know we're lost, thought Julie. Even if it is her fault.

"Look," she said. "Those dolls are from China." She pointed to a man and woman doll dressed in silk. "And that one's from Switzerland. Isn't she pretty?"

"But where are the clocks?" asked Karen, her lip quivering.

"We'll see them soon." Silently, Julie scanned the surrounding shops, trying to remember what had been

71

near the clock shop. She saw Yugoslavian imports and folding canvas boats. Nothing looked familiar. Why hadn't she paid better attention? She led Karen through the crowds around the fountain, trying to think what to do. Up ahead she saw the hot dog stand again. They were going in circles. Fighting off panic, she turned to her sister.

"Karen," she said. "Are you still hungry?" Karen nodded. Julie bought a hot dog for her sister, but she didn't want anything herself. She missed Blanca too much. Why had she ever trusted Karen?

As they walked away from the hot dog stand, Julie saw the Skyride again. She felt her heart lighten just a little. If she kept the Skyride on her left, they would come to Boulevard West.

A few minutes later, she heard the sound of ticking clocks. Their mother looked around as they came up beside her. "Where's your father?" she asked. "I thought you were with him."

Suddenly Julie started to giggle. "He wandered off," she said. "Maybe he got lost." Giddy with relief and miserable about Blanca, she began laughing even harder. Karen joined in. Their mother looked annoyed.

"Really, girls," she said. "It isn't funny! How will we find him in all this crowd?"

At that moment, their father reappeared. "Quite a fountain," he said. "The water and music are controlled by a tape." He smiled down at Karen and Julie. "How about lunch in the Space Needle?"

There was a long line of people waiting to go up in the Space Needle. Julie wanted to cry. She had been waiting all summer for this, but now, without Blanca, she almost didn't care.

"Mom," she said. "Karen lost Blanca."

"Oh, dear," said her mother.

Karen's face tightened. "I didn't mean to," she whimpered.

"We'll check the Lost and Found after lunch," her father said.

They crowded into the elevator. As they soared upward, Karen and Julie looked down at the grounds of the World's Fair and the city beyond. Somewhere down there was Blanca. Julie frowned at her sister, but Karen didn't notice. She was gazing out through the glass, dreaming of far away places. Like me, thought Julie. Her misery began to soften. She felt glad that Karen wasn't lost.

Seated in the Space Needle restaurant, Julie looked out across Seattle at the distant Cascade Mountains. As the restaurant turned in its slow circle, the Food Circus, the Science Center and the International Fountain came into view. Beside her, Karen pushed aside her second lunch with an unhappy face.

"Julie," she said. "What if Blanca isn't in the Lost and Found?"

This time Julie didn't mind her sister's question. "It's okay," she said softly, meaning it this time. "Think of the places Blanca might go. Switzerland or Mexico or even China!" Looking down at the World's Fair, she began to imagine where her little horse might travel next.

If it isn't a box, some kid drops you! I ended up behind one of the booths. When the World's Fair was over, one of the workmen found me. I was put into a box again with two old coats and an umbrella. Boring! There I I stayed until I was given to a family of Laotian refugees. . . .

73

9

1970's

Jump Rope Friends
Amone's Story

Amone (ah-MOAN) hopped from one foot to the other. "It's my turn to jump," she said. "Hurry or the recess bell will ring."

Phoua (POOH-ah) and Sengchanh (song-KAHN) adjusted the long loop of rubber bands around their ankles. They faced each other, their legs a little apart, the stretchy loop pulled tight into a rectangle between them.

"Now," said Phoua.

Amone jumped into the space between the rubber bands. She jumped on one foot. She jumped on both feet. As she moved, the wooden horse in her pocket bounced against her side. She jumped out, and back in again. Her long black hair swung forward, and she pushed it back from her face. She hooked her foot under one strand of the rope, then jumped over the other.

"Watch out!" Sengchanh reached out to catch a red rubber ball that came bouncing across the playground. She missed. The ball hit Amone just as she was jumping out.

Knocked off balance, Amone twisted as she fell. She

By Chris Gustafson

felt the sting of one of the rubber bands as it snapped and broke.

"I'm sorry, Amone."

Amone looked up and saw Lisa, an American girl from her afternoon class.

"The ball got away from our four-square game. Are you okay?" Lisa smiled at Amone. She reached out a hand to help her up.

Amone ignored Lisa's hand and scrambled to her feet. "Okay." She slipped one hand into her pocket to make sure her horse wasn't broken. No. He was okay, too.

The recess bell rang, and Lisa ran off carrying the ball. Her legs look so long, thought Amone, watching the taller girl. She seems friendly. What would it be like to have curly brown hair that bounces when you run?

Phoua wound up the rubber band rope and stuffed it in her pocket. "I can fix it," she said. "Who is that girl?"

"She's in my afternoon 4th grade class." Amone made a face. "I don't like that class. Everyone talks very fast in English. I don't have any friends. Too many new things! I like to stay in the bilingual class." She touched the horse in her pocket again. She carried him everywhere. He was old and familiar, not new and strange.

"I like to go to the 5th grade class in the afternoon." Sengchanh opened the heavy school door and held it for the other two.

"That's because you and Phoua go together. I have to go to my class alone. There's no one from the bilingual class there."

"There's Thavong (thah-VONG)." Sengchanh put her hand over her mouth and laughed.

"He's a boy!"

"Maybe he wants to be your friend," Phoua teased as

they hurried to their room.

Amone got to her seat in bilingual class just as her teacher began to speak.

"The semester is almost over," said Ms. Turnbull. "All of you have improved very much in your English. After next week, you will be going full time in the regular classroom. I am very proud of the progress you have made in reading and writing English. Most of you are speaking very well, too."

As she listened to her teacher, Amone felt tears trying to push their way out of her eyes. She made fists of her hands and rubbed her eyes to hold back the tears. She looked around at all the familiar faces in the class. I feel at home here, she thought. I want to stay.

"For our final project, next week I want each of you to give a short talk in English in front of our class. You may bring something from home to talk about if you like."

For the rest of the morning Amone tried to study, reading English and writing in her workbook. But unpleasant thoughts marched like a column of soldiers through her mind. I have to leave this class. I have to leave. Ever since I left Laos (LAOW-os), I am always starting over again.

The classroom door was open, letting in a hot greasy smell. Amone wrinkled her nose. School lunch. American food was hard to get used to.

When Ms. Turnbull dismissed the class for lunch, Sengchanh and Phoua waited for Amone at the door. "Go on," she told them. "I'll be there soon." She walked up to her teacher's desk.

"What is it, Amone?" asked Ms. Turnbull.

Amone looked down. Her voice was quiet. "My English is not good yet. Not for the regular class."

"You're doing fine, Amone. Just as well as the others."

"The American children will laugh at me."

"Yes."

Amone glanced up quickly at Ms. Turnbull to see if she was joking, but her teacher's eyes were serious. "You're right, Amone. Sometimes they might laugh at you. But you need to have confidence in yourself." Ms. Turnbull patted Amone's shoulder. "I'm sure you can do it."

But Amone wasn't sure. She didn't want to leave the bilingual class. As she walked toward the lunchroom, Amone patted her wooden horse. Maybe, she thought, there is some way I can stay.

After lunch, Phoua took the jump rope out of her pocket and knelt down on the playground. She carefully knotted the ends of the broken rubber band back together. "My turn first."

Amone faced Sengchanh and Phoua jumped between them. "I don't think I will do well on my English speech," Amone said. "Then maybe I can stay in Ms. Turnbull's class."

"You can't stay," Sengchanh told her. "That's silly."

"Besides, we won't be there." Phoua jumped out. "A new bilingual class will come. Lift the rope up," she ordered. "I didn't miss."

Amone and Sengchanh moved the rope up so it was around their knees. "I'm tired of new things," said Amone. "I want to stay."

Phoua began to jump again, higher now.

Amone saw Lisa, the brown-haired girl from her afternoon class. She stood a little ways away, watching Phoua.

"What's that called?" asked Lisa.

78

"Chinese jump rope," Sengchanh answered. "Do you want to try it?"

"Sure. Do I have to start that high?"

"No," Sengchanh said. "You show her, Amone. She's in your class."

Phoua took Amone's end, and she and Sengchanh pushed the rope down around their ankles.

Amone looked up at Lisa. "Like this." Her feet moved quickly between the ropes, jumping in, jumping out. She hooked one side over the other, then leaped up, her feet clear.

"Your turn," she told Lisa.

Lisa put one foot between the ropes. Slowly, she did a one foot jump. A two foot jump. Then she tried to hook one side over and tripped.

"Oh!" Amone put a hand out to steady her. "I'm so clumsy," Lisa said, laughing. "But I want to learn. It looks easy when you do it."

"Watch me again," said Amone. "Then you can have another turn."

"Thanks." Lisa looked right at Amone and smiled. Amone looked down. Then she looked up and smiled too.

"Next recess I'll try to get the long ropes. Do you want to do Double Dutch with me?" Lisa asked.

"Yes. Please." Amone's voice was soft. But she felt her heart give a little bounce, like a red rubber ball. Maybe, she thought, when I go to the regular class I will have a friend. Two friends, she told herself. Lisa and my little horse.

All during the next week Amone's class gave their speeches in English. Amone waited until the very last day.

"Your turn, Amone." Ms. Turnbull nodded at her.

Amone stood up and slowly walked to the front of the

room. She turned around to look at all the faces of her friends. Phoua smiled at her. Amone tried to smile back. In her hands she clutched her wooden horse.

"When I came to America," she began, "it was winter, and very cold. The plane trip frightened me. I didn't know how to eat American food. I was tired. Everything was new. But our sponsors helped us find a place to live. They gave my family a bag of warm coats and some toys. This horse was in the bag. I felt happy to have him, because I had to leave my toys behind to come to America. He is old and many other children have loved him. He is a beautiful horse.

"For a long time I was sad because America is so different. But some new things can be good. I came to this school. I made new friends in this class. And last week I made a new friend in the regular class."

Amone finished. She sat down. When she let go of the wooden horse, her hands were shaking. I'm glad I did my best, she thought.

"Very good, all of you," said Ms. Turnbull. "I've enjoyed having you in my class. You know you can always come back to me and ask for help if you need it."

Amone's eyes moved to the clock. Ten more minutes until recess. Then she and Lisa could play Chinese Jump Rope. And if Lisa got the long ropes they could practice Double Dutch.

 *That fall Amone and her family drove east over the mountains. We were going all the way to Spokane! But at a fruit stall in Yakima, Amone dropped me. What did I tell you? Dropped again! I lay behind the fruit stall all winter. Then one day ashes fell from the sky. . . .*

80

10
1980's

A Gift From The Mountain
Eduardo's Story

Clouds of dusty ash flew into the air as Eduardo (ed-WAR-doh) swept the brick patio. "It's not fair, Amigo (ah-MEE-goh)," he said to the small dog who lay in the shade watching him. "I must give up my whole afternoon to get ready for my sister's party. Elena's (el-LAY-nah) birthday is not until tomorrow. Why must I do all this today?"

Eduardo finished sweeping and put the broom back in the shed. A papier mache (PAY-per MAH-shay) donkey stood on the shelf looking back at him. Bright colors flashed purple and crimson as a shaft of sunlight touched it. "And look at her piñata (pin-YAH-tah), Amigo. It is beautiful." Eduardo sighed. The piñata was filled with candy and toys, ready for tomorrow's party. "I did not get a piñata for my birthday, Amigo. I didn't get anything. And all because of the Mountain!"

That was not quite true, a little voice reminded him. His mother had given him Amigo for his birthday, and he loved the dog very much. But he had not had a party.

By Peggy King Anderson

Eduardo went back outside the shed. He knelt down for a moment to scratch Amigo's ears. He remembered well the morning of his eleventh birthday. It was May 18th, five long months ago. That morning Mount St. Helens had erupted, sending clouds of choking ash from many miles away, toward his town of Yakima.

The whole world had turned dark, or so it seemed, and none of his friends could come to his party. For the next few weeks, everyone had been busy, trying to clean away the ash, and after that it seemed they had all forgotten about Eduardo's birthday.

And now Elena was having her party, with five friends coming.

Amigo stood up suddenly and sniffed in Eduardo's pocket. "I have nothing for you, my friend, but I'll see if Mama has a bit of chorizo (cho-REE-so) left from breakfast." Eduardo loved the hot spicy sausage and Amigo loved it too, as long as his water dish was handy.

His mother was busy in the kitchen, with bowls and pans all over the counter. Clouds of flour flew into the air as she hastily mixed the bowl of batter. "Eduardo," she said, as he scooped up a bit of chorizo from the pan on the stove, "I need some more apples for the cake."

He went outside to the small orchard and picked five apples. Elena would have his mother's delicious tarta de manzana (TAR-tah day mon-SAH-nah) for her birthday. Inside him a great resentment was growing. He was mad at his mother and he was mad at the Mountain. "I know it's silly to be mad at a mountain," he said to Amigo. "But that's the way I feel."

When he took the apples to the kitchen, his mother was not there. He left them on the counter and hurried out.

"Eduardo!" It was his mother calling again. He

84

ducked behind the barn. He would pretend he had not heard. Let Elena do whatever needed to be done. After all, it was her birthday!

From the barn he could see the back of the fruit stand out by the road, and his Uncle Rosario (roh-SAH-ree-oh) busily stacking apple boxes. His uncle looked up as he approached. "Eduardo!" he called out cheerfully. "You are just in time. I have found something, and I am giving it to you!"

Eduardo forgot his anger then, and ran the last few steps. His uncle grabbed him in a big bear hug. "I knew I could make you smile. Here, what do you think of this? I found it this morning when I moved that pile of old boards to put out this new crop. A customer must have dropped it there last fall. Who was it now?"

His forehead creased with thought, Uncle Rosario reached behind a pile of apples and handed Eduardo a small wooden horse. Then his uncle's face brightened. "Ah, I remember. That little Asian girl. She was traveling to Spokane with her family. Now what was her name? It rhymed with Ramon (rah-MOAN). Amone. I am certain it was Amone."

Uncle Rosario looked pleased. He prided himself on remembering his customers. But Eduardo felt disappointment settle over him like the cloud of dusty ash that settled around his feet. The horse was ugly, and dirt still clung to it. "It's a toy for a small child, Tio (TEE-oh). I'm eleven now, you know." Even though we didn't celebrate my birthday, he thought.

"But Eduardo, look closely," his uncle said. "Can you not tell this horse is very old? I am sure it was carved long ago, before you were born. This horse has been a gift to many children." His uncle beamed as he handed it to Eduardo.

It is still ugly, Eduardo thought, but he said nothing.

There was the sound of a car engine down the road and Uncle Rosario looked up. "Quickly, Eduardo. Wash off the apples. Perhaps we will have a customer."

Eduardo put the small horse in his pocket, and ran to get the spray bottle. He went down the row, squirting the apples that lay piled in red mounds. Rivulets of gray dust ran down their sides. You, Mountain, Eduardo said to himself. See the extra work you've made for us?

The car stopped, and a young man jumped out and strode over to the stand. "I'll take five pounds of apples," he said, giving Eduardo a quick smile.

"And where are you going in such a hurry?" Uncle Rosario asked.

"I'm headed for Mount St. Helens. I'm a scientist. We think there may be another eruption soon."

"No!" Eduardo said, and was embarrassed when he realized he had spoken aloud. The man looked down at him.

His uncle put a hand on Eduardo's shoulder. "The mountain erupted on Eduardo's eleventh birthday."

"Then you will never forget May 18, 1980," the man said.

"I don't want to remember it," Eduardo said. "I have seen the pictures. The Mountain destroyed everything."

"We thought that at first," the man said. "But we were wrong. Already there are fireweed and blue lupine blooming on the sides of the mountain, and many of the small animals have returned. We even saw a herd of elk just north of Spirit Lake the other day!"

His uncle looked thoughtful. "We were worried about our apples too, because of the ash, but our harvest is even better than last year."

Eduardo felt anger rising in him. "But the apples are

86

covered with the ash. We have to work hard to clean them over and over again. Everyone is so busy they have had no time for . . . for other things."

Like my birthday party, he thought. And the anger inside him grew bigger. He folded his arms and stood looking sullenly down at the ground. He felt his uncle's surprise at his words. I don't care, he thought. I'm angry at the Mountain. Finally I have someone to tell, someone who knows all about this Mountain.

The scientist put a hand on his shoulder. "Eduardo, I have something to show you." He walked over to his car, and returned holding a beautiful vase. Its colors glowed purple and blue, as if a strange light came from within.

Eduardo kept his arms folded, but he knew his eyes must tell the scientist that he found this vase beautiful. The man smiled. "The colors are from a special glaze made with ash from the mountain, Eduardo."

How could the ugly ash make something so beautiful? Eduardo stared at the vase.

The man held it out to him. "Take it. It's a birthday present for you, so that you'll feel some joy when you re-member that day."

Eduardo took the vase. He walked slowly back to the orchard, with Amigo following him. He turned the vase in his hands, seeing its glowing colors. His mother loved beautiful things too. He would show it to her. He re-membered then that she was back at the house, rushing to get everything done before his sister's birthday tomor-row.

"I'll go back and help her, Amigo. I don't feel so angry anymore." As he walked toward the house, some-thing poked him. He looked down and saw the wooden horse sticking out of his pocket. He smiled then, think-ing of his uncle's words about the horse being a gift to many children. "I'll give it to Elena," he said to Amigo, "for her birthday."

As he neared the house, he saw the piñata swinging gently from the branch of the apple tree by the patio. "Why is it hanging already, Amigo? If we have wind tonight it will blow down before the party."

He saw his mother then, standing by the back door. She called to him. "Eduardo! Where have you been? I have been looking for you."

But she didn't look angry. She was smiling, and as he hurried up, he saw the apple cake, with eleven candles burning on it.

Manuel, Jason, and the other boys from his class poured out the back door, pushing each other and laughing. "Surprise!" they yelled.

Eduardo stood still. He felt first a lump in his throat and then a great happiness.

His mother had not forgotten his party after all. She hurried over to him and hugged him. "I am sorry it took so long to do this, Eduardo." She stood back and looked at the vase. "Where did you get this?" There was awe in her voice. "It is beautiful."

Eduardo held it up so all could see. "It is a gift from the Mountain," he said.

 *I didn't see much of Eduardo's party, because I was in his pocket the whole time. But Elena's birthday party was fun! After she unwrapped me and her other presents, the children took turns hitting the piñata with a stick. When it broke, candy rained down. All of the children scrambled to pick it up.*

I like Elena. She plays with me every day and always puts me in a place where I can see what is going on. She calls me Caballo (cah-BY-oh) which is Spanish for "horse." I have had a lot of names and I have been a friend to many children. But my real name is N'uks-Cha-Ska-Ha, the horse of many adventures. I wonder where I will travel next?

Glossary

amigo—Spanish word for friend.

bilingual—able to speak and understand two languages.

Boeing—company in Seattle, Washington, which develops and manufactures airplanes.

boulevard—a broad street.

camas—plant whose root-bulb was eaten by Pacific Northwest Indians.

chaff—husks or outer covering of grain, separated off by a threshing machine.

Chelan—Pacific Northwest Indian tribe and language.

chorizo—spicy Mexican sausage.

Entiat—Pacific Northwest Indian tribe and language.

evacuated—removed from a place.

expedition—trip made for specific purpose such as exploration.

Galapagos—group of islands off the northwest coast of South America.

header—harvesting machine which cuts the top "heads" off the grain.

hula-hoop—plastic hoop swung around the body by the hips.

irrigate—supply water for crops through ditches or sprinklers.

Laos—a country in southeast Asia.

Laotian—person from Laos.

latrine—a pit dug in the ground to be used as a toilet.

Methow—Pacific Northwest Indian tribe and language.

missionaries—people who travel to another culture or area to share their religious beliefs and often perform charitable works such as education or health care.

moccasins—soft leather shoes worn by Native Americans.

nisei—Japanese word for an American-born Japanese person whose parents were born in Japan.

Okanogan—Pacific Northwest Indian tribe and language.

orthopedic—branch of medicine which deals with bone and joint problems.

papier-mache—strips of paper coated with glue and used to mold and make things.

parfleche—bag or pack made out of tough rawhide.

parlor—room used for receiving guests.

phobia—extremely strong, irrational fear caused by a specific thing or situation, often so strong that the person is unable to move or think.

piñata—hollow animal or figure made out of papier-mache and filled with candy and treats. It is hung from a high place during a party, and blindfolded children try to break it with a stick.

polio—disease which is often crippling; most people today receive shots to keep from getting it.

Puyallup—city south of Seattle, Washington.

quarantine—to keep a sick person and his or her belongings away from other people so that the disease will not spread; often the belongings are burned.

riffle—a ripple on the surface of water.

satellite—a man-made object, launched by rockets, which circles the earth.

Sauk—name of a logging camp and a river in the Cascade Mountains in Washington.

Spacearium—space exhibit at the World's Fair in Seattle, Washington.

Sputnik—first satellite in space, launched by the Soviet Union.

squall—sudden storm of wind and rain.

suiyape—Wenatchi word for "white" or "Caucasian."

Tarheel—slang nickname for a person from North Carolina.

tarta de manzana—apple cake.

threshing machine—a large harvesting machine used to separate seeds and grain from chaff and straw.

tio—Spanish word for uncle.

vaccination—shot given to keep a person from getting a certain disease.

Wenatchi—Pacific Northwest Indian tribe and language.

winch/winching—a machine used to lift or pull by winding rope with a handle around a spool.

whittle/whittling—carving wood with a knife.

OTHER FINE BOOKS
FROM PARENTING PRESS, INC.

The Decision Is Yours Series

These choose-your-own-ending books offer a chance to think about real life problems before they happen to *you*. What the character does is up to you...and then you get to see what happens when he or she makes that choice.

Finders, Keepers by *Elizabeth Crary*

You and your friend Jerry find a wallet that belongs to your neighbor. Jerry wants to take some money and buy ice cream. You're not so sure.

Jerry calls you a chicken. What will you do? The decision is yours!
$3.95 paper, 64 pages, illustrated

Bully on the Bus by *Carl W. Bosch*

Nick, a big fifth grader and the school bully has promised to beat you up today.

Will you go to school? Will you fight him? The decision is yours!
$3.95 paper, 64 pages, illustrated

Making the Grade by *Carl W. Bosch*

You like soccer practice much better than homework and this term's report card shows it.

How can you show two D's and an F to your parents?

Will you "forget" to take your report card home? Ask your friend Karen for help? Talk to your teacher? The decision is yours!
$3.95 paper, 64 pages, illustrated

Biographies for Young Children

These books tell the stories of spunky girls who grew up to make important changes in our society. Read what they did when they were children and how they decided to be the women they were.

Elizabeth Blackwell: The Story of the First Woman Doctor
by *Shari Steelsmith*

Elizabeth had an exciting and unusual childhood; besides helping her father free slaves during the Civil War, her parents also let her study with her brothers. That was something hardly anyone had ever heard of before.
$5.95 paper, 32 pages, illustrated

Harriet Tubman: They Called Me Moses by *Linda D. Meyer*

Harriet was born a slave in Maryland, but she didn't let that state of affairs last very long! Her life-story is one of adventure, danger and excitement as she became one of the most famous conductors on the Underground Railroad. *$5.95 paper, 32 pages, illustrated*

Juliette Gordon Low: Founder of the Girl Scouts by *Shari Steelsmith*

Read about Juliette's active childhood, her willingness to take risks, and her tremendous work with the Girl Scouts.
$5.95 paper, 32 pages, illustrated